RAINBOW magic ®

The Green Fairies

Special thanks to
Narinder Dhami

ORCHARD BOOKS
338 Euston Road, London NW1 3BH
Orchard Books Australia
Level 17/207 Kent Street, Sydney, NSW 2000

A Paperback Original
First published in 2009 by Orchard Books.

A CIP catalogue record for this book is available
from the British Library.

ISBN 978 1 40830 478 5
5 7 9 10 8 6

Printed in Great Britain

The paper and board used in this paperback are natural recyclable
products made from wood grown in sustainable forests. The
manufacturing processes conform to the environmental regulations
of the country of origin.

Orchard Books is a division of Hachette Children's Books,
an Hachette UK company

Lily
the Rainforest
Fairy

by Daisy Meadows

ORCHARD

The fairies must be in a dream
If they think they can be called 'green'.
My goblin servants are definitely greenest
And I, of course, am by far the meanest.

Seven fairies out to save the Earth?
This idea fills me full of mirth.
I'm sure the world has had enough
Of fairy magic and all that stuff.

So I'm going to steal the fairies' wands
And send them into human lands.
The fairies will think all is lost

Defeated again, by me, Jack Frost!

Contents

Food From the Forest

"Look, Kirsty," Rachel Walker called as she hurried through the trees, "I think I've found some wild onions!"

"Oh, great!" Kirsty Tate, Rachel's best friend, ran to join her, swinging her basket. The two girls were on a nature walk in the forest near their holiday cottage on Rainspell Island, where they were spending the half-term week with their families.

Rachel and Kirsty knelt down and peered at the onion plants. They had long thin leaves and greenish–white flowers, and in the middle of the flowers were little onion bulbs.

"The Junior Naturalist class we went to this morning was fun, wasn't it, Kirsty?" Rachel said with a smile. "I never realised there were so many things to eat growing wild on Rainspell Island. Have you got the soup recipe the teacher gave us?"

Kirsty took a leaflet labelled *Mushroom Soup* out of her basket.

"Remember, Jo told us that we should only take as much as we need," Kirsty reminded Rachel. "Otherwise the plant won't be able to seed itself, and then it might die."

Rachel checked the recipe ingredients. Then carefully she removed some of the onion bulbs and put them in Kirsty's basket. The girls had already collected some sprigs of sweet-smelling wild thyme, and other herbs.

"Now we just have to find some mushrooms, and we can make soup for dinner tonight, with our mums' help!" Rachel jumped to her feet. "We must remember to check the booklet about mushrooms that Jo gave us, Kirsty, because we have to be sure the ones we find aren't poisonous."

"Isn't it amazing how many different plants and animals there are in the forest?" Kirsty remarked as they wandered off along the path again.

"I know," Rachel agreed. "It was so interesting this morning when Jo explained how all the plants and animals and birds rely on each other, and on the forest, for their food and shelter."

Kirsty glanced around. The leaves on the trees were turning red, gold and yellow, and squirrels were leaping busily about, collecting nuts to store for the winter. "I love Rainspell," Kirsty said happily. "I'm so glad we came back." Rachel nodded in agreement.

Rainspell Island was really special to Rachel and Kirsty because it was where they first became friends, *and* where they first met the fairies!

No one else knew about Rachel and Kirsty's magical friendship with the fairies. In the past, King Oberon and Queen Titania had often asked for the girls' help whenever they had problems with Jack Frost and his naughty goblin servants. But this time it had been Rachel and Kirsty's turn to ask the fairies for *their* help.

The girls had been shocked when they returned to Rainspell Island to find litter on the beautiful golden beach, so they'd used their special lockets to visit Fairyland and ask the king and queen to help clean up the human world.

The king and queen had made seven
fairies-in-training the Green Fairies for
a trial period. If they completed their
allotted tasks, they would become
permanent. Rachel and
Kirsty had been
thrilled to find
out that
these fairies
would try
to make
the world
a cleaner,
greener
place. But
they knew
that humans
had to
help, too.

But just as the Green Fairies were about to be presented with their new wands, Jack Frost and his goblins had zoomed in on an ice bolt. The goblins had grabbed the wands, and then Jack Frost's icy spell had sent them spinning away into the human world.

Jack Frost was trying to prevent humans from becoming greener, but Rachel and Kirsty were determined to find the wands and return them to the Green Fairies so that they could start their important work.

"I wonder if we'll find another wand today?" Kirsty remarked, as the girls made their way through the trees.

"Remember what Queen Titania always says," Rachel replied. "We have to wait for the magic to come to *us*! But four of the wands are safely back in Fairyland now, at least."

"And we know that fairy magic can't sort out all our environmental problems," Kirsty added. "We humans have to do everything we can to help as well!" She pointed at a tree just ahead of them.

"Look, Rachel, isn't that a silver birch?"

"Yes," Rachel agreed, admiring the tree's beautiful silvery trunk. "Jo showed us one this morning, didn't she? And look," she went on, "there are some wild flowers growing at the foot of it."

As the girls were looking at the tiny purple flowers, Kirsty felt a drop of rain splash onto her face.

Suddenly more rain began to pour down
on them from the darkening sky.

"Quick, Kirsty!" Rachel called
to her friend. "We can shelter
under that cluster of
trees over there."

The girls
ran
towards
the trees
and
huddled
underneath
them.

"That's
better!" Kirsty said,
shaking her damp hair out of
her eyes. "The rain's really coming
down now, Rachel."

Rachel was about to reply when suddenly she cried out in delight.

"This is amazing!" She pointed down at the grass at her feet, and there was a circle of gleaming white mushrooms.

"Brilliant!" Kirsty laughed. "Isn't it lucky that we came to shelter here?" She opened the leaflet their teacher had given them, and checked the pictures carefully. "I think these mushrooms are safe to eat, but we'll ask our mums, too," Kirsty said at last. "They'll go beautifully in our soup!

I'll just collect as many as we need, and no more."

Kirsty bent down to pick a few mushrooms. But then she gave an exclamation of surprise.

There, sheltering under one of the mushrooms, was Lily the Rainforest Fairy!

Amazing Rainforest

As Rachel bent to look, Lily fluttered
out from under the mushroom. She
wore green wide-legged trousers, and an
off-the-shoulder green top, and her long
black plaits flew out behind her as she
hovered in front of Rachel and Kirsty.

"Girls, I'm so happy to see you!" Lily announced joyfully, turning a cartwheel in the air. "I'm on the trail of my wand, and there's no time to lose. Rainforests everywhere need my help!"

"Do you know where your wand is, Lily?" asked Rachel eagerly.

"Is it close by?" Kirsty added.

Lily's face fell a little. "My wand isn't on Rainspell Island," she replied. "It's far away, in a rainforest!"

Rachel and Kirsty looked dismayed.

"As you know, girls, I only have a little fairy magic without my wand," Lily went on. "I have just enough to take the three of us to the rainforest, but unless I find my wand, I may not have enough magic to bring us home again!" She looked solemnly at Rachel and Kirsty. "I'll understand if you don't want to take the risk and come with me."

"We'll come," Rachel said, a determined look on her face, and Kirsty nodded in agreement.

After all their many adventures with
the fairies, the girls were confident that
they'd be able to help Lily outwit the
naughty goblins and get her wand back!
They also knew that time stood still in
the human world while they were in
Fairyland.

Lily looked relieved. "Thank you, girls,"
she cried. "We'll go right away."

Their hearts thumping with
excitement, Rachel and Kirsty linked
hands as Lily snapped her fingers.
Immediately, a faint mist of glittering
fairy dust floated down around
the girls. They shrank down
to fairy-size and soft,
fluttery fairy wings
appeared on
their backs.

Then Kirsty and Rachel noticed that the raindrops still falling from the sky were beginning to sparkle and shimmer. Soon the raindrops became so bright and dazzling that the girls had to close their eyes. The next moment they felt themselves whizzing through the air.

"Welcome to the rainforest, girls!" Lily laughed.

Rachel and Kirsty could feel the heat on their skin before they even opened their eyes. When they did so, both girls gasped aloud in utter amazement.

The three of them were hovering among the tree tops of the rainforest, high above the ground. The trees were growing so close together, their branches intertwined to form a thick, leafy canopy. Hot, dazzling sunshine shone here and there through the gaps. Long ropes of vines hung from the trees, swaying lazily in the slight breeze.

The air was warm and damp, and all the leaves, exotic flowers and ripe fruits were wet with drops of moisture that made their colours glow.

Rachel and Kirsty could see bananas, coconuts and mangos growing near them. They could also hear the noisy songs of tropical birds, as well as the calls of animals hidden among the trees.

"This is the most amazing place I've ever seen!" Rachel murmured, her eyes wide.

"And the hottest!" added Kirsty, as the three

friends fluttered down to the rainforest floor.

Lily smiled. "The rainforest is *very* hot and wet," she explained. "It gets lots of sunshine and rain every day, and that's why it looks so green and beautiful." She pointed up at the canopy of overlapping branches and leaves above them. "You might be surprised to know that most of the plant and animal life in the rainforest is up there in the canopy, not down on the ground."

"Really?" Rachel began, but then she gave a gasp of surprise as a golden-coloured monkey suddenly jumped out from the middle of a tree near her. Chattering away to himself, the monkey began to 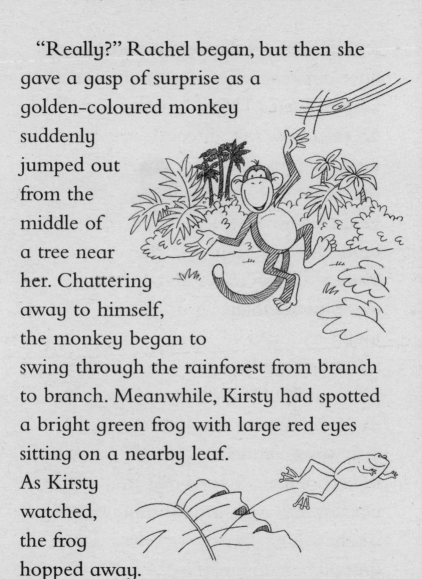 swing through the rainforest from branch to branch. Meanwhile, Kirsty had spotted a bright green frog with large red eyes sitting on a nearby leaf. As Kirsty watched, the frog hopped away.

"The animals that live in the canopy have different ways of getting around," Lily explained. "They fly, they hop, they jump and they swing from branch to branch! Come and have a closer look."

Rachel and Kirsty followed Lily as she zoomed up to the tree tops, zipping neatly between the interwoven branches. The girls saw lots of birds, insects, flowers and fruit in the canopy that were strange and unfamiliar. There was so much to see, they hardly knew where to look next!

"The rainforest is very important because it provides a home for many different kinds of plants and animals," Lily explained. "It's also very important for humans because the trees help to produce the planet's oxygen."

"This is fantastic!" Kirsty sighed happily as a beautiful red and blue dragonfly fluttered past. "But we mustn't forget that we came here to look for your wand."

"You're right," Lily agreed. "And I can sense that my wand is around here *somewhere*. We'll start searching for it right away."

But at that moment Rachel thought she heard a noise above the cries of the birds and animals. She frowned. Had she *really* heard something, or had she just imagined it?

"What's the matter, Rachel?" asked Kirsty.

"I thought I just heard something rather odd," Rachel replied. "Can you and Lily hear it?"

Kirsty and Lily listened hard, but at first they couldn't hear anything unusual. Then all of a sudden, a loud noise echoed through the canopy.

It was a creature screeching anxiously at the top of its voice!

Goblins in Bulldozers

Rachel, Kirsty and Lily were horrified by the distressed call.

"The sound is coming from over there." Kirsty pointed to a thick clump of trees. "I think we should go and see who it is!"

"Good idea," Rachel replied, and the three friends flew towards the trees.

"Let's split up and take a look around," Lily suggested in a low voice. "It'll be quicker that way. But be careful, girls!"

Kirsty fluttered up higher to search the
canopy while Rachel and Lily began
looking among the trees lower down.

Suddenly Lily cried out.

"Over here, girls!"

Kirsty and Rachel zoomed over
to her. Lily drew them out of
sight behind a large leaf
and then pointed to the
next tree. On a
branch sat a big
scarlet and
blue parrot,
squawking
loudly.

"I wonder
what he's saying?"
Rachel whispered.

"Let's go and ask him!" Lily replied.

Kirsty, Lily and Rachel flew towards the parrot. The bird looked rather surprised when they landed on the branch next to him and screeched again.

"A little magic will help us understand what he's saying," said Lily. She snapped her fingers and a few glittery sparkles drifted around the parrot.

"Hello, I'm Lily the Rainforest Fairy," Lily went on. "And these are my friends, Kirsty and Rachel. What are you trying to tell us?"

The parrot fluffed out his bright feathers, looking very upset. "Green hurts trees!" he said.

Lily, Kirsty and Rachel looked bewildered.

"Help save trees!" the parrot screeched, flapping his wings frantically.

Lily shook her head, baffled. "I'm afraid I don't understand what you're trying to tell us. Can you *show* us what you mean instead?" she asked.

The parrot nodded. Instantly he spread his wings and zoomed away through the trees.

"Quick!" Lily gasped. "Or we'll lose him!"

The three friends dashed after the parrot as fast as their wings could carry them. They ducked and dived between branches and leaves, occasionally coming face-to-face with surprised birds and monkeys.

"There he is!" yelled Rachel, catching a glimpse of scarlet and blue ahead of them.

Lily, Rachel and Kirsty rushed towards the parrot. Luckily, he was slowing down so they could catch up with him a little.

"Look, he's stopped in that clearing," Kirsty said. She could see the parrot perched on the branch of a tree.

"But what's that terrible noise?" Rachel asked.

Lily and the girls flew closer. To their amazement, they saw five big bulldozers roaring around the clearing. The bulldozers were knocking into each other and banging into the trees. As Kirsty, Rachel and Lily watched, the smallest tree was hit particularly hard by one of the bulldozers and it toppled over. There were shrieks and cries of fear as panic-stricken birds flew out of the branches, and monkeys leapt to safety in nearby trees.

"This is terrible!" Kirsty exclaimed. "We must stop them!"

Rachel glanced at the bulldozer drivers who were wearing hard hats. She looked more closely and spotted green pointy ears and noses peeking out from under the hats.

"The drivers are goblins!" Rachel gasped.

Then Kirsty noticed something else.

One of the goblins was holding a stick, and every time another bulldozer got too close, the goblin leant out of his cab and poked the other driver with it. As he did so, a very faint cloud of fairy dust surrounded the stick.

"And that goblin has Lily's wand!" Kirsty exclaimed.

Fruit Storm

"Now I understand why the parrot kept saying *Green hurts trees!*" Lily exclaimed. "My rainforests are in danger because humans are chopping down the trees – and now the goblins are destroying them, too!"

"We must stop them, *and* get the wand back!" Rachel said anxiously.

The three friends whizzed into the
clearing, keeping high above the
bulldozers. They flew over to the parrot
who was still sitting on the branch,
his wings drooping miserably.

"We're going to do everything
we can to stop the goblins
destroying the rainforest,"
Lily told him. "Now why
don't you go home,
where you'll be safe?"

"Thank you," the
parrot squawked,
and he flew away.

"STOP!" Kirsty
yelled as one of the
bulldozers crashed
into the tree where the
parrot had been sitting.

"They can't hear us over the noise of the engines," said Rachel. "Let's fly down lower."

Quickly, Lily and the girls zoomed towards the bulldozer of the goblin holding the wand.

"Stop!" Rachel shouted, as they hovered around the driver's cab. "What are you doing?"

The goblin looked up at them and scowled.

"Playing bumper cars, of course!" he retorted, poking his tongue out at them.

He reversed his vehicle and rammed into a tree with a jolt, before racing towards one of the other bulldozers.

Lily and the girls dashed after him.

"Please give my wand back!" Lily shouted to the goblin, as she, Rachel and Kirsty landed on the window of his cab. "I need its magic to look after rainforests all over the world, and to help all the creatures that live in them!"

Before the goblin could say anything, two other goblins in bulldozers rumbled straight towards him.

The three bulldozers all crashed into each other, and the impact sent Lily, Rachel and Kirsty tumbling off the window. They hurtled through the air, but landed safely on a large, soft leaf.

"Girls, are you OK?" Lily asked.

"We're fine," panted Kirsty, "but we *must* get the goblins off these bulldozers!"

Lily nodded. "They're disrupting the ecosystem of the rainforest," she said solemnly. "That means they're putting all the plants, animals and trees in danger."

"Let's fly up to the canopy," Rachel suggested. "It'll be quieter, and maybe we can come up with a plan."

Lily and the girls fluttered higher, and landed on a tree laden with large, round, green and yellow fruits. The goblins were still charging around in the bulldozers and whooping gleefully whenever they hit a tree or each other.

"What can we do?" Lily asked sadly. "I don't have enough magic to stop them."
Rachel and Kirsty looked around for something to help them.

"But all I can see are leaves, flowers and fruit," Rachel said to herself. She stared at the fruits hanging around them. She didn't know what they were, but she could see that the young fruits were green, while the ripe ones were bright yellow. Some of them were rotting on the branches. Rachel pushed one and it fell to the ground, just missing the nearest bulldozer.

"Oh!" Rachel gasped aloud. "I think I have an idea. Kirsty, Lily, follow me!"

Rachel zoomed off through the
canopy. Puzzled, Kirsty and Lily flew
after her. But they soon realised what
Rachel was up to when they saw her
gently knocking down the big ripe,
rotten fruits onto the goblins
below them. The fruit
landed on the
bulldozers,
splattering
their
windscreens
with pulp
and seeds.

"Great
idea, Rachel!" Kirsty said as
she and Lily started knocking
the fruit down too. "If the goblins can't
see, they'll have to stop!"

As fruit rained down on the bulldozers,
the goblins shrieked with annoyance and
drew to a halt. They all switched on their
windscreen wipers, and began clearing
the mess away so that they could see.
Rachel, Kirsty and Lily tried desperately
to knock down more and more fruit, but
it was very difficult to do it quickly
because they were so small.

"This isn't working!" Rachel exclaimed
in dismay, shaking her head. "We'll have
to try something else."

Meanwhile, the goblins had cleared
their windscreens and were revving up
their engines again. Clouds of black
smoke were belching from their exhaust
pipes. As Kirsty watched, her face
suddenly lit up.

"Now *I* have an idea!" she announced.

Animal Army

"Maybe we can still use fruit to stop the bulldozers," Kirsty went on.

"But we know that won't work," Rachel sighed.

Kirsty grinned. "We can use the fruit in a *different* way," she replied, and she pointed to a bunch of bananas down below them. "By stuffing it in the bulldozers' exhaust pipes! I saw it work in a film once."

"Are you sure?" Rachel asked, "that sounds a bit dangerous."

"But we've got to stop those bulldozers," said Lily, thoughtfully. "We'll take out the bananas as soon as the bulldozers' engines stop. That will make sure no permanent damage is done."

Lily and the girls flew down to the clearing, keeping well away from the bulldozers. A few magic fairy sparkles made Kirsty and Rachel their normal size again, and then the girls crept over to the banana tree. Standing on tiptoe, they pulled down a few bananas from the big clump hanging on the tree.

Quickly Lily whizzed over to the bulldozers and flew around them trying to distract the goblins, who stopped their machines to swat at the fairy.

Meanwhile, Rachel and Kirsty crept into the clearing and each pushed a banana into the bulldozers' exhaust pipes. When Lily saw that the girls had blocked all the pipes, she flew high into the canopy. The goblins immediately put the bulldozers in gear, and the machines began to move slowly forward again.

But the bulldozers had hardly moved at all before they started spluttering and choking to a halt. The goblins looked puzzled.

"What's going on?" the goblin with the wand roared, hopping down from his cab. "My bumper car's stopped!" Suddenly he spotted Rachel and Kirsty darting across the clearing. "It's those interfering girls again!" the goblin shouted angrily.

The other goblins jumped down from their bulldozers, and they all charged at Rachel and Kirsty. But Lily was quicker. She dashed towards the girls and clicked

her fingers. Immediately Rachel and
Kirsty shrank down to fairy-size, and the
three of them flew up
quickly into the air
out of the goblins'
reach. Lily waved her
arms again and the
bananas magically
popped out of
the bulldozers'
exhaust pipes.

"We don't know
what kind of trouble the
goblins will cause with my magic
wand!" said Lily. "We mustn't get too
close to them."

"Give us the wand back, please!"
Rachel called to the goblins below them.
"It belongs to Lily, not you."

The goblin with the wand chuckled.
"Catch me if you can!" he sneered. He
jumped up onto his bulldozer, grabbed one
of the long vines hanging from a tree and
swung away through the rainforest. The
other goblins did the same.

"They're getting away!" Kirsty cried in
dismay, as the goblins swung speedily from
vine to vine.

"After them!" Lily yelled.

The three friends gave chase.
The goblin with the wand
glanced over his shoulder and
saw Rachel coming up fast
behind him. Grinning, he
gave the wand to the goblin
swinging past him, like a
runner in a relay race.
Rachel made a desperate

grab for the wand, but the second goblin immediately handed it to a third, who swung right away from her.

"Keep your eye on the wand, girls!" Lily called, as the third goblin passed it neatly back to the first goblin.

It didn't take the goblins long to get the hang of swinging on the vines, and soon they were moving along incredibly fast. Rachel, Kirsty and Lily tried their best to fly faster themselves, and also to keep track of the wand. But it was very difficult, because the five goblins passed it back and forth so often.

"We need help!" Lily panted when the goblins had got quite far ahead of them. She snapped her fingers, and Rachel and Kirsty saw some fairy sparkles dancing in the air.

A few moments later, the girls heard
rustling noises in the leaves behind them.
Glancing over their shoulders, they were
amazed to see a whole army of animals
and birds appear. There were and
orang-utans and other different kinds of
monkeys. There were macaws and toucans
and lots of brightly coloured birds, as
well as lizards, snakes and large and
small insects.
Right at the
front was the
scarlet and
blue parrot
Lily and
the girls
had met
earlier.

"Thank you for coming, everyone," Lily said gratefully. "We must catch those naughty goblins and get my wand back!"

Chattering and cooing, whistling and chirping, the animals and birds of the rainforest swung, jumped, hopped, wriggled and flew after the goblins.

"They're much quicker than us!" Rachel laughed, as the animal army easily overtook them.

"But how will they stop the goblins?" Kirsty wondered. Then her eyes widened as she watched the goblins swinging from vine to vine. "Oh! Maybe we could use the *vines* to trap them!"

All Tied Up

Lily nodded. She zoomed over to the parrot and whispered something to him.

Rachel and Kirsty watched as all the animals and birds rushed after the goblins, grabbing long ropes of vines in their teeth, beaks or paws on the way. Some went in one direction, some in another and some of them even managed to get in front of the goblins so that they were surrounded on all sides.

"Now!" Lily called.

Instantly the animals swooped forward holding the vines, and surrounded the goblins.

"Hey!" the goblin with the wand shouted furiously as the animals and birds began neatly wrapping the vines around them. "What's going on?"

In just a few moments all the goblins were neatly trussed up like a vine-wrapped

parcel. They yelled and struggled, but
they were tied too tightly to get free.

"Well done, everyone!" Lily laughed.

Rachel and Kirsty flew over and took
the wand from the
goblin, who glared
sulkily at them.
They carried it
to Lily, and the
instant she
touched it, the
wand shrank
back to its fairy
size. Rachel and
Kirsty beamed at
each other.

"Now, you've caused
enough trouble for today!" Lily
said, pointing her wand at the goblins.

A stream of fairy dust shot towards them, and the vines that held them prisoner untied themselves. "It's time you went home to Jack Frost's castle."

Grumbling bitterly, the goblins swung themselves away through the trees and out of sight.

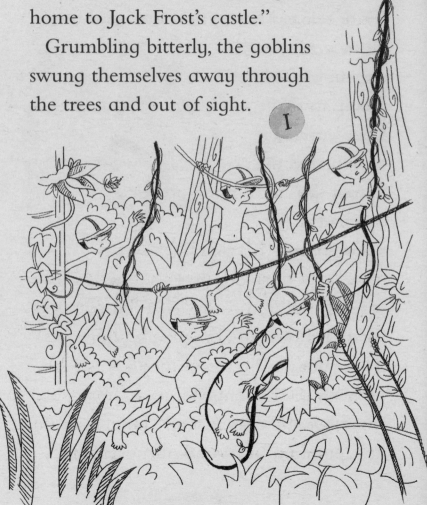

Lily turned to
the girls. "Thank
you for being
brave enough to
come with me,"
she said, smiling.
"And now I
have my wand, I
can send you safely home. But first,
I must get rid of those horrible
bulldozers!"

The friends hurried back to the
clearing. Quickly Lily waved her wand,
and used her magic to heal the damaged
trees and stand them upright again.
Then, with a shower of magic dust, she
reduced the huge machines to fairy-size.
"At least the loggers won't be able to do
any more harm for a while," she said.

"I must get back to Fairyland, girls,"
Lily said, "and I shall tell everyone there
how wonderful you've been today! I
couldn't have got my wand back without
you. Now I can begin my work of
protecting the rainforests – and there's so
much to do!"

"I wish we could do more to help,"
Kirsty sighed. "The
rainforests are so
beautiful, but
they're also so far
away from where
we live."

"You can help
by telling other
people about the
rainforests,"
Lily suggested.

"Let them know more trees are being
cut down every day, and that we *must*
stop it."

"We will," promised Rachel.

Lily smiled and pointed her
wand at the girls.
"Goodbye!" she called
as a stream of fairy
sparkles lifted
Rachel and
Kirsty off
their feet
and whirled
them into
the air.

In the blink of an eye, Rachel and
Kirsty found themselves back in the
forest on Rainspell Island. The rain had
stopped now, and the sun was peeping
through the clouds.

"But it's not as warm as the
rainforest!" Kirsty laughed,
kneeling down
to place the
mushrooms in
her basket.
"Wasn't
that a
fantastic
fairy adventure,
Rachel?"

Rachel nodded. "And,
like Lily said, we can
tell everyone all

about the trees in the rainforest being destroyed." She thought for a moment. "Maybe we could get in touch with a school in one of the rainforest countries, like Brazil, and start a tree-sponsoring scheme?"

"Oh, that's a great idea," Kirsty exclaimed, picking up her basket. "And we could organise some fundraising events at our schools. We could have one where everyone dresses up as rainforest animals!"

Rachel laughed. "There are lots of things we can do," she said, "but right now our mission is to recycle these mushrooms into a delicious soup!"

Now it's time for Rachel and Kirsty
to help...

Milly the River Fairy

Read on for a sneak peek...

"Brrrr, it's definitely colder than
yesterday," Rachel Walker said, as she
and her best friend Kirsty Tate strolled
through Rainspell Park. "I can't believe
we were so warm on the beach at the
start of the week – and today we're all
wrapped up in our woollies!"

Kirsty grinned at Rachel. "And *I* can't
believe we were swimming in the sea
with Coral the Reef Fairy a few days
ago," she said in a low voice. "Imagine
how freezing cold the water must be
right now!"

Rachel shivered at the thought. "She'd have to use a *lot* of fairy magic to keep us warm today, wouldn't she?"

The two girls smiled at each other as they walked on through the park.

It was the autumn half-term, and they were both here on Rainspell Island for a week with their parents. Rainspell Island was the place where Kirsty and Rachel had first met, and they'd shared a very magical summer together…and now this holiday was turning out to be every bit as magical.

"Oh, I do love being friends with the fairies," Kirsty said happily, thinking about all the exciting adventures they'd had so far. "We really are the luckiest girls in the world, Rachel."

"Definitely," Rachel agreed.

Golden-brown leaves were tumbling from the trees in the park every time the wind blew, and she noticed just then that some of the trees were already bare. "Well, it's definitely windy enough today to sail our boats, anyway," she said, as a yellow horse chestnut leaf floated down and landed at her feet. She glanced at the paper boat she was holding. Both girls had made one each back at their holiday cottage that morning. "They're going to whizz along with this breeze behind them."

"Here's the lake now," Kirsty said as they rounded a corner and saw the stretch of blue water ahead of them...

Read Milly the River Fairy to find out
what adventures are in store for Kirsty and Rachel!

Meet the
Green Fairies

Rachel and Kirsty must rescue the Green Fairies'
magic wands from Jack Frost, before
the environment is damaged!

www.rainbowmagicbooks.co.uk

Meet the fairies, play games
and get sneak peeks at
the latest books!

www.rainbowmagicbooks.co.uk

There's fairy fun for everyone on
our wonderful website.
You'll find great activities, competitions, stories and
fairy profiles, and also a special newsletter.

Get 30% off all Rainbow Magic books at
www.rainbowmagicbooks.co.uk

Enter the code RAINBOW at the checkout.
Offer ends 31 December 2013.

Offer valid in United Kingdom and Republic of Ireland only.

Win Rainbow Magic Goodies!

There are lots of Rainbow Magic fairies, and we want to know which one is your favourite! Send us a picture of her and tell us in thirty words why she is your favourite and why you like Rainbow Magic books. Each month we will put the entries into a draw and select one winner to receive a Rainbow Magic Sparkly T-shirt and Goody Bag!

Send your entry on a postcard to Rainbow Magic Competition, Orchard Books, 338 Euston Road, London NW1 3BH. Australian readers should email: childrens.books@hachette.com.au New Zealand readers should write to Rainbow Magic Competition, 4 Whetu Place, Mairangi Bay, Auckland NZ. Don't forget to include your name and address. Only one entry per child.

Good luck!

Meet the Ocean Fairies

Naughty goblins have smashed the magical conch shell! Kirsty and Rachel must restore it so that the oceans can have harmony again.

www.rainbowmagicbooks.co.uk